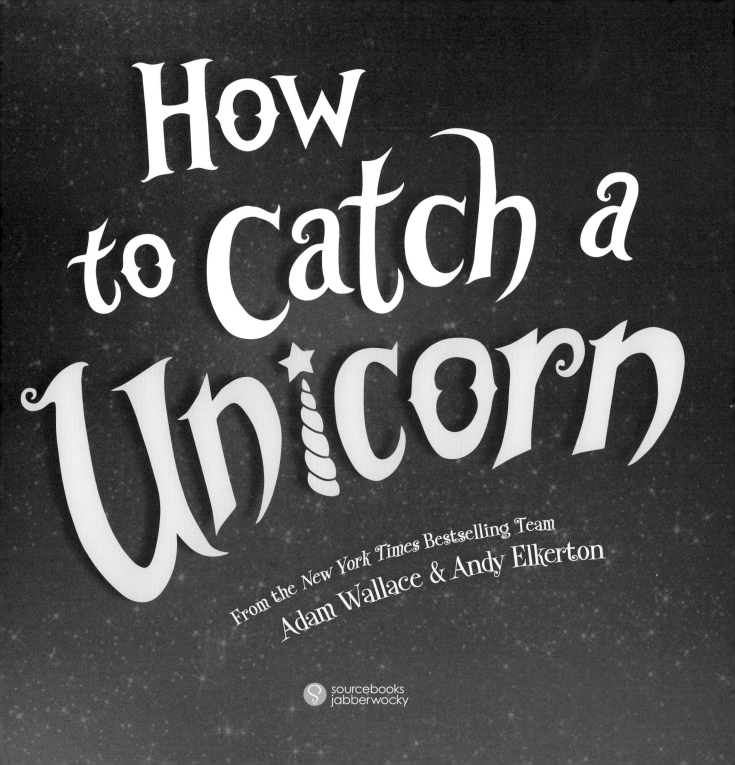

How to Catch a Unicorn

From the New York Times Bestselling Team

Adam Wallace & Andy Elkerton

sourcebooks
jabberwocky

On this bright and shiny morning,
I want something fun to do,
so I'm riding on a **RAINBOW**
and I'm heading to the zoo!

The kids think they have spotted me–
I thought I'd blend in here!
I cannot let them catch me
or my magic will **disappear!**

Butterfly House

Nocturnal House

Luckily my animal friends,
from the zebra to the ape,
are all on board to help me.
They will make sure I **escape!**

First, I see my stripy cousins,
but then I have to *fly*.
As much as I like lemonade,
I have to say goodbye!

KICK!

Unicorn
Lemonade

I dodge the plastic parachute
being launched from down below.
I do a spin and leave a trail
of ✦GLiTTER✦ as I go.

I **chill** with all my penguin pals
but these traps are everywhere!
I'll head to the nocturnal house—
I hope it's safe in there!

Wow, this room is super dark—
I'm glad I'm a **Unicorn**.
Who knows what I might walk into
without my magic horn?

Now I'm off to see more friends.

It's time to shrink my size!

But it sure is hard to see in here

with all these butterflies!

Baby Animals Petting Zoo

Unicorns EAT for FREE

My nose smells something super sweet
coming from the CAFÉ.
Oh yum! I snag a little bite
before I fly away!

Next up, I go to where it's hot
and where there's lots of scales!
The *snakes* and *lizards* help me, though,
with their clever use of tails!

I'm big again and with more friends—
these monkeys make me laugh!
But I would have been caught easily,
if not for the giraffe!

What's over there? A paddle boat?
This could be lots of fun!
I would stay in the water,
but my friends are roaring, "RUN!"

While visiting my beaver friends,

I spy a welcome sight!

My true friends come to save the day

with their bold, brave, beaver BITE!

The gift shop makes the perfect place
for your elaborate trap,
but LUCKY for me, there's a decoy
to safely take the rap!

zoo-minoes

I had fun with my friends today—
the zoo has been a blast!
You tried your best; your traps were smart,
but unicorns are *FAST!*

Now it's time for me to go
and maybe take a nap.
Meanwhile, keep on trying, kids—
I'll be back to best your **traps**.

Copyright © 2019 by Sourcebooks • Text by Adam Wallace • Illustrations by Andy Elkerton • Cover and internal design © 2019 by Sourcebooks • Sourcebooks and the colophon are registered trademarks of Sourcebooks • All rights reserved. • The art was first sketched, then painted digitally with brushes designed by the artist. • Published by Sourcebooks Wonderland, an imprint of Sourcebooks Kids • P.O. Box 4410, Naperville, Illinois • 60567-4410 • (630) 961-3900 • sourcebookskids.com • Library of Congress Cataloging-in-Publication Data is on file with the publisher. • Source of Production: Shenzhen Wing King Tong Paper Products Co. Ltd., Longuang District, Shenzhen, China • Date of Production: April 2021 • Run Number: 5021904 • Printed and bound in China. • WKT 24